2024 Best Short Stories

Riversong Contest

Edited by Neela Tudurí-Kłepfisch

An Imprint of Sulis International Press

Los Angeles | Dallas | London

Published by Riversong Books
An Imprint of Sulis International
Los Angeles | Dallas | London

www.sulisinternational.com

Contents

Preface i

Story Without End 1
Khalil Kubiak

Slouching Towards Oblivion 7
Samuel Offerman

1972 17
Derek O'Gorman

shapes that don't belong 63
Adelaide Prentiss

The World Grows Wild...69
Red Semiakina

Between the Lines...75
T.J. Thompson

Zapatos 83
Sylvia G Vega

Preface

I am honored to present this third volume of winning stories3 for the Riversong Short Story Contest, which showcases the talents of new and unique story writers.

We received an impressive 42 short stories, spanning a diverse range of genres. Many of these stories were exceptionally well-crafted, making it challenging for our judges to select just a handful of winners.

Among the winning stories are literary fiction, poetry, contemporary fiction, poetry, and fantasy. These stories come from writers as young as 17 and as old as 65, and they hail from all corners of the globe.

"Story Without End" by Khalil Kubiak is an intriguing experiment that delves into the mind of an individual trapped in a bustling city. The constant noise and buzz gradually drive the protagonist to the brink of madness, creating a thought-provoking exploration of the human psyche.

"Slouching Toward Oblivion" by Samuel Offerman offers a slice-of-life story that delves into the themes of attitude, judgmentalism, and self-deception. Through the characters' interactions, the author challenges readers to confront their own biases and assumptions.

Derek O'Gorman, an Irish short story writer, presents "1972," a captivating tale set during a sweltering summer in France. A group of Irish female footballers finds themselves as guests of a contemplative order of nuns near Paris. This period of reflection, revelation, awakening, and life-altering decisions unfolds, creating an emotionally resonant narrative.

"shapes that don't belong" by Adelaide Prentiss is a poetry winner that captivates with its simple structure and evocative imagery. The reader is left to interpret the meaning of this word painting, allowing for a deeper connection to the poem.

Red Semiakina's poetry winner, "The World Grows Wild," uses a straightforward vocabulary and rhythmic structure to explore the experience of intentionally getting lost in a jungle. This symbolic journey serves as a metaphor for life's uncertainties and the transformative power of exploration.

"Between the Lines" by T.J. Thompson presents a modern love story that unfolds entirely through text messages. This unique narrative style challenges readers to engage with the story on a deeper level, as they decipher the emotions and intentions conveyed through the characters' digital interactions.

Our grand finale story winner is the captivating "Zapatos," penned by the talented Sylvia G. Vega. This beautifully written narrative follows the journey of a newly arrived Cuban family residing in the bustling city of New York. The word "zapatos" holds diverse meanings for different individuals, adding depth and richness to the story.

We extend our heartfelt gratitude to our esteemed Contest Judges:

- Sheri Addison, a skilled freelance editor
- Anthony Holmes, the esteemed Director of Publishing at Sulis International Press
- Mira Innes, a renowned literature blogger
- Mark McFaddyn, an accomplished editor at Sulis International Press
- John Sparks, a distinguished editor and reviewer at *Historical Fiction Review*

On behalf of Sulis International Press and Riversong Books, we extend our warmest congratulations to Khalil, Samuel, Derek, Adelaide, Red, T.J., and Sylvia.

Neela Tudurí-Kłepfisch
Miami, Florida

Story Without End

Khalil Kubiak[*]

The city pulses, a throbbing heart of concrete and steel, breathing in the noise of life below, and he stands, a solitary figure, watching the ebb and flow from his thirtieth-floor perch. The window glows, a fractured screen against the night, a gaping maw of glass and metal, through which the world spills out—a river of lights, a flood of human souls, a torrent of thoughts, desires, and despair. All those flickering points in the dark, tiny stars in a vast, indifferent universe, each one a story, a struggle, a fleeting moment of joy or sorrow, all of it crashing and clashing in a symphony of chaos that reverberates in his chest.

He stares into the abyss of the city, the distant sirens wailing like lost souls, the honking horns weaving a tapestry of impatience, of urgency, of lives tangled in the throes of existence. Ah, the city, a beast of burden, a

----

*Khalil Kubiak is a schoolteacher from the London area. Khalil has been writing short fiction and poetry since he was 12 years old. He has been published in university publications, local magazines, and contests.

gnarled hand grasping for dreams, clawing at the sky, and yet he is locked in this cage, this glass box, suspended above the fray, where every heartbeat is an echo of the lives below, muted but insistent, like the bass line of a haunting melody that refuses to fade.

What time is it? The clock on the wall blinks, a digital eye watching him watch. He can't remember when he last ate. Did he eat? Or did the day slip away in a haze of thought, in a fog of memory and forgetfulness? He looks down at the remnants of his last meal, a cold slice of pizza, the grease congealed, the cheese hardened. The fridge hums softly, a lullaby of mechanical life, but it's too empty, too hollow to offer comfort, just like this place. He can feel the hunger gnawing, a beast within him, but the thought of leaving this spot, stepping into the streets, seems impossible, too daunting. What could he face out there? Faces, faceless crowds, all moving in a dance he no longer knows the steps to.

Oh, but the people! He can see them moving below, little figures rushing to and fro, their lives intersecting for fleeting moments, a kiss here, a fight there, laughter spilling out of a bar, echoes of joy mingling with the stink of cigarettes and cheap whiskey. It's a carnival of existence, and he is the ghost, hovering above it all, neither participant nor spectator, just an observer of the dance, the intricate ballet of humanity, spinning in a dizzying whirl, a cyclone of emotion and energy that threatens to pull him in but never does. It is better this way, isn't it? To remain untethered, floating in the ether, avoiding the sharp edges of connection that cut deep and bleed.

The phone vibrates again on the table, a siren call in this desolate expanse. He hesitates, his fingers hovering above it, the screen glowing with the promise of interaction, of life beyond these walls. It could be her. It usually is. Her words, so filled with warmth and color, a splash of brightness against the gray monotony of his days, her laughter ringing like chimes in a breeze. She wants him to come to her, to escape this urban cage, to feel the grass beneath his feet, to breathe air not tainted by the scent of exhaust and regret. But he can't. He won't. What is there for him outside these walls? Nothing but more noise, more faces. The thought sends a shiver down his spine. So he ignores the buzz, lets it fade into the silence, another message lost in the ether.

Outside, the lights twinkle like stars in a manufactured sky, the buildings rising like cliffs, looming over him, casting shadows that stretch and yawn, and he can feel the weight of them pressing down, smothering him with the very air that surrounds him. There's something alive in those shadows, something that watches, something that waits. He thinks of the stories he's heard, the whispers of things that lurk in the dark corners of the city, creatures born of despair and madness, and he shudders, pulling the curtains closed as if to block it all out. But the darkness seeps through the cracks, thick and oily, a palpable presence that wraps around him, suffocating.

He paces the room, the floorboards creaking beneath his weight, a reminder of the life that pulses through this structure, a heartbeat beneath his feet. How long has it been since he felt the warmth of the sun on his face? Since he breathed air that wasn't tinged with the scent of decay? The walls seem to close in, their white paint peeling like old skin, revealing the bones of the building beneath. He touches the wall, feels the rough texture beneath his fingertips, and for a moment, he imagines it alive, pulsing with memories of those who've come before him, their laughter, their tears, all absorbed by the very bricks that surround him.

The city doesn't sleep. It churns and twists, a restless beast, and he can hear the thrum of its heart. He presses his ear against the wall, listening for the whispers, for the murmurs of those who live around him. The couple in 29B fighting again, their voices rising like a storm, breaking against the silence. The woman in 32D, always crying, always alone, her sobs like the tolling of a bell, ringing out into the void. He knows their stories, has pieced them together from fragments, from the echoes that bounce off the walls, and it leaves a taste of bitterness in his mouth. They are all trapped, all tethered to this place, this high-rise prison.

He can't escape the thoughts that swirl like smoke in his mind, each one curling around the other, creating a haze that's challenging to see through. What if he's just like them? What if he's lost, wandering through the labyrinth of his making? The city is a reflection of his mind, a tangled web of dreams and nightmares, each street a path he has walked down before, each alley a reminder of choices made and unmade, of moments that slipped through his fingers like sand. He feels the weight of it all, the burden of existence pressing down like a vice, and he wonders if it's always been like this, or if something shifted, something broke within him.

There's a sound, a scratching at the edge of his awareness, a noise that pulls him back to the present. The vent! It's happening again. The noise, persistent and insistent, like a whispering voice trying to break through. He freezes, heart pounding, every instinct screaming to run, to hide. The sound isn't just in his head; it's real, a scuttling, a scratching, something moving through the walls, crawling closer. He steps back, breathing shallow, the surrounding shadows stretching, bending, warping into shapes that tease at the corners of his vision. No, it's just the building settling, he tells himself. Just the old pipes groaning. But the sound continues, a soft scuttling, like a rat—or worse.

He stares at the wall, heart racing, mind racing faster, drowning in thoughts that crash against each other like waves in a storm. What if it's not a rat? What if it's something worse? The stories he's heard come flooding back, tales of things that crawl in the dark, things that don't belong. He can't remember where he heard them —was it a podcast? A book? Or just the chatter of strangers in a bar? It doesn't matter. The fear is real, palpable, and it gnaws at his insides, twisting and turning, feeding on his anxiety.

He grips the edge of the table, knuckles white, willing himself to breathe, to think. But the noise grows louder, more insistent, a scratching that echoes through the hollow cavity of the wall. His imagination spins wild images of what could be lurking just beyond the plaster, dark eyes peering out, teeth glistening, waiting for him to falter, to let his guard down. He can feel it creeping closer, feel the air grow thicker, heavier, pressing against him, suffocating.

He can't stay here. He needs to get out, to escape the confines of this high-rise prison, to break free from the invisible chains that bind him to this place. But the thought of stepping out into the chaos, the noise, the faces that don't recognize him, that terrifies him just as much. It's all too much. The weight of it all—the city, the shadows, the sounds—crushes him, and he can feel the walls closing in, the darkness wrapping around him like a shroud.

He takes a step back from the wall, and then another, retreating into the center of the room, away from the noise, the gnawing terror. He closes his eyes, tries to shut it all out, to breathe, to gather himself, but the scratching persists, clawing at his sanity. He can feel the walls trembling with the weight of it all, the fear and anxiety swirling in the air like a storm, and he knows he's losing himself, losing grip on reality.

He sinks to the floor, back against the cold wall, fingers tangled in his hair, heart racing like a trapped animal. The scratching becomes a heartbeat, pulsing in time with his own, a sinister rhythm that drags him deeper into the abyss. He thinks of the people below, moving, living, laughing, their lives a blur of color against the monochrome of his own existence. He wonders if they ever feel this way, this crushing weight of despair, or if they too are trapped in their own minds, battling unseen demons behind closed…

Slouching Towards Oblivion

Samuel Offerman*

Kerry spotted Susan approaching the coffee shop door. She observed Susan scanning the room. Soon, Susan noticed Kerry and made her way over with a friendly wave.

"Hi, Kerry," Susan greeted her with a smile. "I'll get my coffee and be right back." Kerry nodded in acknowledgment.

The coffee shop wasn't particularly crowded, and Kerry soon returned with her coffee. "It's so warm today," Susan remarked. "Perhaps coffee wasn't the ideal choice."

"Yes, it is quite warm," Kerry replied. "How did your weekend go?"

Susan set her cup down, settled into the chair opposite Kerry, and placed her purse on the ground beside her.

*Samuel Offerman is an independent editor and researcher for fiction, nonfiction, working with authors, organizations and companies. This is his first published fiction story.

"Oh, it was generally good. Mostly. Mick was supposed to fix the shelves in the garage after his golfing trip on Saturday, but he was so exhausted that he didn't manage to do it. I was quite upset for a while, but I eventually realized I was overreacting. This golfing trip with his brother had been meticulously planned for months. They returned much later than anticipated. The shelves aren't that significant—I had been feeling unwell and had a short temper. We reconciled later. He even took some of the blame, though it wasn't entirely his fault."

"I understand how it can be," Kerry nodded in agreement. "Dan used to make promises to me and consistently fail to deliver. Before our divorce was finalized, he had promised to fix the faucet he had broken before the kids returned from college. He never did. We were married for seven years; he knew that I had a problem with people who make promises and don't keep them. It all stems from when my grandmother passed away when I was eight years old. She raised me —my mother was absent for most of my childhood. When Grandma died, I felt a sense of abandonment that has never left me."

"Yes, I remember you telling me that." Susan looked away as someone came in through the door.

"I thought Dan was different," Kerry continued, "and that he understood my abandonment issues and wouldn't be so self-centered, but he turned out to be like every other guy I ever dated."

Susan took a sip of her coffee and made a face. "Oh, my, this is not right. Too sweet."

"Yeah, sometimes this place doesn't make their coffee hot enough. Probably because some idiot burned themselves and sued them. They don't know how to make *real* coffee, either, like they do in Italy. Dan and I were in Italy a few years ago, remember? Did I tell you he went to the bank while we were there to get some money and got lost coming back? I was in the hotel room waiting for an hour! I told him how much I hated being left alone, but he didn't pay attention when we walked to the bank and got lost. I was mad."

"I am going to have them fix this. Be right back." Susan scooted her chair back and headed to the counter.

One of the waiters was cleaning up the table next to Kerry. She had seen him before—she came here often. He was young—younger than Kerry—with dark features that always caught her attention. "How are you today?" She always tried to be nice to people she saw regularly.

He looked up. "Doing well. How are you?"

"I'm fine. Though my friend's coffee wasn't made right, so she went to get another cup. You guys are usually pretty good at that, but no one is perfect, huh?" She smiled.

"Oh, yeah," he answered, looking back down at the table he was wiping. "We have been very busy today. I've been here since six. One of the workers didn't show up, so it left us all short-handed."

"Oh, don't you hate that? Why can't people be responsible? So many people don't even think of others. During my freshman year at college, I had two roommates who used to always leave the dorm a mess. When

I tried to speak with them about it, they ganged up on me and made life miserable for the rest of that year. I was so glad to get out of that room."

He finished up cleaning off the tabletop. "Yes, well, what can you do? Just keep doing what you are supposed to do. Have a good day." He turned to clean another table.

Kerry took a sip of her coffee, set the cup down carefully, and looked up as Susan returned.

"Do you know him?" Susan asked, nodded towards the retreating waiter.

"No. Well, I see him in here all the time. But I don't really know him. We were just talking about irresponsible people. Maybe I talked too much, though. Did it seem like he left abruptly? He said something about one of the workers not showing up, and I told him about my college roommates who hated me and left our dorm for me to clean up all the time. I've told you about them. Was I talking too much?"

"No, I am sure he just had to work."

"I don't know. I think I made him uncomfortable. Do you think he thought I was criticizing the worker who didn't show up? Perhaps it was his friend. Or his girl-friend. And I shot my mouth off. Oh, how embarrass-ing." She shook her head. "I am so dumb sometimes."

"I think you are overanalyzing. He just told you someone didn't show up for work, chatted a bit, then went back to doing his job."

Kerry sat looking at her cup for a moment. "I guess you are right. I do that all the time. It's all the times in my life I have been treated badly by others. Makes me think people are always thinking badly of me."

The door opened, and an elderly man came in, spotting the two women almost immediately. "Hello, girls! What a nice day it is."

"Hello, Mr. Sandy. How are you?" said Susan. "Have a seat?"

"Well, yes, for a moment, that would be nice. On my way to the hardware store, thought I'd get a coffee to go. You know, this weather reminds me of when I used to live in Arizona. Sometimes these warm days would hit in the middle of winter! Like a breath of fresh air, so to speak, reminding us that the winter cold would not last forever, no matter how tired we got of it."

As he finished speaking, a woman with three small children bustled by on their way out, a chaotic dance of voices, cups, bags, arms, and legs. One of the older children bumped Mr. Sandy's chair. He jumped, then laughed when he saw the cause. He watched the group of kids as they all tried to squeeze through the door at once. He gave a little laugh.

"Ugh, that's just what we were talking about before you came in," Kerry said. "That kid and the woman didn't even say, 'excuse me.' People just don't take responsibility for their actions anymore. They are so caught up in their own world."

"Oh, I don't know," said Mr. Sandy pleasantly, "they're just kids enjoying life."

"Maybe. I don't know. I was just telling that guy over there—" Kerry nodded towards the counter "—about my college roommates treating me badly. Some people said they were just caught up in their own lives and didn't realize what they were doing to me. But I know they didn't like me. In fact—"

Susan's cell phone rang.

"Sorry," she said as she fumbled for it in her purse. "Hi, sweetheart…yes, I am at the coffee shop now…sure…no, no problem at all…love you, too. Bye." She closed the phone.

"That was Mick. He needs me to bring some files from home down to the office. Must go!" She put the phone in her purse and picked it up as she stood. "I'll see you later on, Kerry. Will you be at the church meeting tonight?"

"Yes, I'll see you there."

"Okay." She smiled at Mr. Sandy. "Good to see you, Mr. Sandy. Have a lovely day."

He half stood and bowed slightly. "You, too, Susan. Say hello to Mick for me."

He sat back down. He and Kerry sat in silence for a moment.

"Poor Susan," said Kerry. "Her husband treats her like a servant."

"Really? I always had the idea that he was very attentive to her. They seem happy."

"Well, appearances can be deceiving. He is very selfish, always getting her to do things for him, and he always has excuses for not doing what she needs. I wish I could help them."

Mr. Sandy sat for a moment. "Hm. I really didn't know that they had troubles."

"It reminds me of my ex-husband. I thought we had such a great relationship at first. It seems like we were partners, you know? Me taking care of him, him taking care of me. But after a few years, I realized that he was totally self-centered. It had all been an act. Even during our divorce, he said he'd fix the faucet he broke, so I wouldn't have to deal with it later. I thought that was nice: in spite of what was happening, he was doing something nice. But he never did. He lied, as usual."

"Well, I am sorry, Kerry. Relationships can be very difficult sometimes."

"Oh, well, it is long over. Many years ago. I have moved on. But it has made it hard for me to trust people—especially men."

"Yes...I can understand," said Mr. Sandy. "Yes..."

After a moment of silence, he moved his chair back. "Well, I really must get on with my errands." He stood and smiled down at her. "Have a good day, Kerry,"

"Thank you, Mr. Sandy. You, too."

*

An hour later, Kerry had read the local paper and was on her third cup of coffee. Her phone rang. She picked it up from the table and looked at the screen: it was her mom. She took a deep breath.

"Hi, mom...I am at the coffee shop...yes, *again*." A long silence.

"That's tonight...yes...at seven...no, I am fine." More silence.

"I don't know. Just a little down, I guess. I'm okay."

"Yes, Susan was just here. It was nice…James? Uh, no…Mom…well…we broke up." She sighed quietly and rolled her eyes."Last week…I don't want to talk about it. You know how it makes me feel…no, it was him. But he wasn't right for me. He was selfish, like Dan." She listened, turning her half empty cup in circles.

"Do we have to talk about this now?" She sighed again and took a deep breath.

"Yes, I am lonely, sometimes, but it is not my fault that everyone I care about abandons me. You and dad divorced, then grandma died, then—"

"—I know she didn't die on purpose, mom. But it still makes me feel abandoned. And then Dan, even though he was a scum and wasn't good for me, he still left me. And my roommates in college, and —" She stopped, then her face red, though she was doing her best to hide the anger in her voice.

"I do not. You just don't know what it is like…Yes, yes, I know. You say that all the time. You just don't understand…okay mom…okay…okay…can we not talk about this now?" She listened again, tapping the edge of the coffee cup.

"Yes. Okay. I'm sorry…Okay. I will call you tonight after I get home…Bye."

Kerry set the phone down on the table and stared at her coffee cup. Slowly she became aware of two women sitting near her, one of whom was talking rapidly and without any pauses. Kerry listened for a while, wondering how the second woman could stay so silent. She listened to the outflow of jabber.

"She just doesn't get it. She is not a good supervisor at all. I don't know why they hired her. I have been there for three years, and could do her job easily and have time left over. She treats me like I don't know what I am doing. Why didn't they hire me instead of making *me* do this on-the-job training? And everyone knows I could do it better, but for some reason, those higher-ups don't like me. I'll never get ahead at that place. And—get this—the other day, she asked me to pick her up some lunch when I was going to get mine. Can you believe that? There has to be some job out there that uses my true talents, and not these people who are so concerned about themselves—did I tell you this?—the other day Karen was getting ready to leave early…"

Kerry sighed to herself. She drank the last bit of her coffee and stood up. Collecting her things, she left the coffee shop, shaking her head.

1972

Derek O'Gorman[*]

A convent rooftop near Paris.
The Summer.

Helen Grace sat forward. She was hot, stifling hot. She looked to her side. Angela Delaney was fast asleep on her portion of the towel they were both sharing. Angela's blouse was lying in a heap where she had tossed it, while Helen's lay neatly folded. At Angela's feet, the football that never left her side. Helen could clearly make out two perfectly formed sunburn lines parallel to each side of Angela's lemon bra straps and the beads of sweat on the tips of her bra cups and underwire.

Helen checked herself and thanked God for her mother's side of the family. Helen's sallow skin was beginning to form a chestnut hue. She pushed her own bra forward for a peek of the virgin white skin of her own

---

[*]Derek O'Gorman is a teacher in Cork City, Ireland. He has written for stage and had his work has been produced on RTE Radio and adapted for film for the Cork Midsummer Festival. This story appears in a collection of Derek's short stories entitled *On the Third Day* (2024).

breasts. She smiled to herself. Would the rugby boys back in Callan find an erotic glimpse of white more alluring or incongruous? She remembered how Danny Walsh had felt cold to the touch and how she had reacted with a startled jump, frightening the living daylights out of the poor young fella into the bargain. She cupped herself. She felt warm. She turned her attention to Angela. Two newly formed red patches were clearly visible on her inner thighs. That wasn't good. She nudged Angela firmly.

"Are you awake?"

"I am now," Angela replied, sitting up groggily.

"You need to be careful," Helen advised; "You know what they say about sleeping in the sun. I had a friend one time, Mags Phelan, and she got burned to a crisp in Dunmore East. Blisters the size of golf balls she got." Helen shuddered at the memory of it.

"And you're telling me this, why? Because?" Angela's tone was filled with annoyance.

"In agony she was."

"And is that all you want to tell me? About Mags Phelan and her sunburn?" Angela continued, barely containing her irritation.

"I'm just saying."

"Good. I'll make note of it," Angela finished sarcastically, and she made to roll over on to her stomach, smoothing her portion of the towel as she did so. Helen adjusted herself also.

"Angela?"

"What now?"

"Nothing."

Angela rolled over on to her back once more, sat up and hugged her knees to her chest.

"Go on, I'm awake now," she said forlornly.

Helen pointed into the distance; "Those workers on that roof there. Do you think they can see us?"

Angela followed the trajectory of Helen's arm with curiosity and sure enough, there they were on an adjoining roof, three workmen with their backs hunched to the sun like mollusks.

"Do you want them to see us?" Angela asked mischievously.

"God no," Helen exclaimed, but Angela had already sprung to her feet and was waving her arms windmill-like in the direction of the men; "Hey over here!"

"Will you stop!" Helen said in panic.

Angela had her back to Helen now. She placed her index finger and middle finger between her lips and released a loud shrill whistle; "They can see us now alright," she laughed, turning back towards Helen.

"Jesus, Mary and Joseph," Helen gasped, ducking down sharply before scrambling to unfurl her blouse. She threw it around herself and began buttoning it up hectically. Angela remained unmoved.

"Do you think those French lads have ever seen a pair of fine strapping Irish girls before?" she guffawed, slapping her own hips; "And a good set of childbearing hips."

"Get down and behave yourself," Helen replied impatiently, but Angela took no notice of this reprimand and commenced to parade herself in a provocative manner;

"And I have it on good authority," she proclaimed with certainty.

"What?"

Angela stopped and pirouetted towards Helen; "That I am well put together."

"Will you give over?"

"With a powerful behind."

"Just cover up or the nuns will have us excommunicated," Helen said briskly, throwing Angela her blouse. Angela caught the top and in one movement fired it back with interest: "'Tis up here they should be instead of praying all day and baking bread."

"Shh, they'll hear you."

"Shur, they won't be able to say anything anyway. Isn't that against their religion?"

"And for your information, it's Matins and Vespers. It's not just prayers."

"Do you not find it strange, though?" Angela probed; "All these women under one roof and not a peep out of them?"

Helen held out the blouse once more; "I don't, now will you please put that on."

"Yes mammy!" Angela snapped, taking the blouse grudgingly. She put it on slowly and began to button herself up painstakingly. When she had the blouse half done up, she began unbuttoning again with a flourish, humming *The Stripper* with gusto and dancing a series of exaggerated striptease actions.

"Jesus Angela!" Helen responded crossly.

"Alright, alright. We can't have the poor nuns getting overexcited. Bless us and save us," Angela conceded.

She made a quick sign of the cross and finished tying up the garment efficiently. A sense of order descended once more and Helen was contented; "Mick was saying, if it wasn't for the nuns putting us up like this, we wouldn't have been able to play these games at all. There are some Irish nuns here who helped sort it."

"Imagine that, though. Getting away and ending up trapped here instead," Angela answered ruefully; "And he told me that the French crowd were scouting me last night. Introduced me to their coach after the game."

"Did he now?" Helen offered, barely concealing her surprise.

"Talked about me signing professional. Imagine that. Getting paid to play football."

Helen *knew* that was all Angela ever wanted and when she spoke of it, her face would light up in the anticipation of what that might be like for her. Helen also understood such a wrench would have consequences, not least for Bob and Kit, the grandparents who had raised Angela in north inner-city Dublin. That was a subject Angela spoke less of.

"And what did you say?" Helen asked composedly.

"I told him I'd think about it."

"And Bob and Kit?"

"They'll be grand," Angela dismissed; "He told me I was a little flyer."

"And who told you that?"

"Pierre, *toute vitesse,* to be exact."

Helen laughed at Angela's new-found command of the French language and raised her eyebrows quizzically; "Pierre?"

"Yes, their coach. Are you listening to me at all? Do you agree? That I'm a little flyer."

Helen made herself comfortable once more on the towel; "The first time I saw you."

"You don't think I'm too, stocky?" There was genuine concern in Angela's voice.

"I never thought about it."

"Mick says I have a low centre of gravity, perfect, he says for holding up play."

Helen scanned the opposite roof. The men seemed to have maintained working oblivious; "Mick has something to say to all the girls," she said vacantly.

Angela kneeled her left leg on to the towel and thrust her right thigh forward towards Helen.

"Feel that."

"What?"

"Go on," Angela encouraged.

Helen hesitantly took hold of Angela's thigh. It felt smooth and firm.

"Really press on it," Angela instructed.

Angela took Helen's hand in hers and guided her to press down on the flesh. Angela flexed her thigh and Helen could feel the muscular resistance.

"There," Angela said knowledgeably; "Like tree trunks, he says. Well-built."

Helen removed her hands with a start. They had begun to get sticky, so she wiped them off her own thighs as she sat back down: "Well, he is not getting his dirty paws on my thighs! Yuch!!"

"He likes you," Angela said quickly as she stood again.

"Stop, you're giving me the creeps now!" Helen grimaced.

"Really?"

"God no. And you?"

"Mick thinks I can turn on a sixpence. Kept telling Pierre that after last night's game."

Angela made some space for herself; "Throw us that ball there. I'm bored now."

"For you to fall off the roof and break your two legs. I will not."

"Go on. Don't be such a killjoy. Mick says the ball should be an extension of your body. Control, control, control. Just lay it on for me there." Angela signaled for the ball, indicating where she wanted it exactly, but Helen plunged forward to scoop the ball into her chest; "You're not getting it!"

"Says who?" Angela responded sharply, and she made a quick darting motion to snatch the ball from Helen's grasp. The girls laughed instantaneously as they attempted to wrestle control of the football, and Helen was about to squirm her way free with the ball intact when Angela plunged her fingers under Helen's arm-pit and began tickling her. Helen fell back on to the towel, overcome with laughter. "Stop! Seriously, stop! I'm going to be sick!!"

Angela felt Helen's resistance relax, and she stood upright triumphantly, ball in hand. Helen sat up fixing herself on the towel; "You're some witch. That hurt!" she accused, rubbing herself fervently where Angela had grabbed her.

"I'm easy on the eye though," Angela batted back, a smile flashing across her face. She had liked that compliment when she had heard it first. She threw the ball up for herself. It was something all the team agreed on. When Angela and the ball were in full-flow she was indeed spell-binding. Helen shielded her eyes from the sun as Angela took two delicate first touches with her right foot, before shifting the ball effortlessly onto her left thigh. Her face was a study in concentration, arms low by her side, pony-tail bobbing gently behind her in rhythm with the movement of her body. She eased the ball back onto the side of her right foot before popping in naturally up onto her right knee. She then proceeded to interchange her touches from right to left foot, all the while with the ball under consummate control. Helen had seen her perform this movement many times at training, a gentle lofting of the ball up on to her right shoulder where she cushioned it before a final lean forward to secure the ball between her back and the nape of her neck.

But not today. Today, she allowed the ball drop from her right shoulder, and she pivoted at the final moment to smash the ball venomously skywards with her left foot. The ball sailed into the distance.

"Back of the net!" Angela shouted gleefully, and she punched the air in mock celebration.

"Cop on Angela! I'm serious." Helen's voice was filled with agitation.

"And so am I. The French girls play in an organised league, and the best ones can go on and play for their country."

But Helen was no longer paying attention as Angela laid out this potential football pathway for herself. Helen was staring intently into the distance, eyes fixed on the neighbouring roof.

"Jesus, Angela, you really have gone and done it this time!"

*

He was young, tall, and a shock of black unkempt curly shoulder-length hair partially obscured his deep brown eyes. His striped t-shirt was sweat-stained from the work and his work pants was mottled with timber shavings and had an array of pockets from which protruded various tool handles at differing angles. They looked inviting, waiting to be touched. Neither girl had seen teeth so even, teeth that gleamed the way his seemed to, but it was his right hand that drew all their attention. There, balanced perfectly on the upturned palm, was Angela's football.

"Girls. I think this is yours, no?" he held the ball out for closer inspection, his lilting French accent peppering the air.

"Thanks. Got it in one." Angela's response was curt. With that, he lofted the ball gently to her; "You girls are enjoying the good weather?"

"We are, and you?" Angela nodded, securing the ball under her arm.

"Working, fixing the leak."

Angela turned to Helen; "Do hear that, Helen? The nuns have a leak."

"On the roof," he added.

"The best place to have one," Angela smiled.

"Pardon?" His face remained expressionless.

"Ah 'tis nothing. We are only messing with you, fella." Angela's face softened.

He took the opportunity to step closer; "You are the Irish girls, yes? The footballers staying at La Carthusian."

Angela took the lead; "That's us in the flesh. Isn't that right Helen. Gosh my apologies. We haven't even introduced ourselves. You must think we are a right shower." She also stepped forward and, wiping her right on her shorts, offered it to him; "I'm Angela, Angela Grace."

"Pleased to meet you Angela, and I'm Luc, Luc Dugarry," he replied, taking her hand and shaking it politely.

Helen stepped to Angela's side and gave a quick demure wave; "Hi, and I'm Helen."

"Hello Angela and Helen," he chimed, taking a step back once more, his voice warm.

"And do you play football yourself?" Helen asked, folding her arms across her chest, self-consciously.

"A little." Luc ran a hand through his tousled hair.

"And what else do you do when you are not fixing roofs?" Angela added.

"I study at the Sorbonne in Paris. My first year. I wish to become a teacher and travel also."

"Wow." Helen's eyes shone with excitement, and Angela threw her a look; "And have you been to Ireland yet?" Angela asked calmly.

"Not yet. I wish to go some day. I spent two months in London last summer to improve my English, and this summer I fix roofs." Luc tossed his head back resignedly.

"And when you do come, we will show you round," Helen interjected enthusiastically.

"I would like that."

"No bother," Helen gestured, looking him directly in the eye.

"And what do you girls do when you are not playing football on the roof?"

Angela raised her hand before Helen could answer; "Me? I work in a factory in Dublin. It's not what I want, but it pays well. Most of the team are there and the manager," she offered up dolefully. Angela's take on her own situation was not a new revelation for Helen, and she stepped beyond her, within touching distance of Luc now; "But what Angela really wants to do is play football for a living in France. Don't you Angela?"

"Amazing. You must be truly excellent." A smile spread across Luc's face.

"Angela can turn on a sixpence."

Luc's gaze was totally set on Helen now: "And what about you? *Pouvez-vous allumer un six pence?*"

"Sorry?" Helen looked perplexed.

Luc laughed; "And now I'm...how do you say? Only messing with you." He patted Helen playfully; "And what would you like to do?"

Helen felt herself blushing; "I would also like to go to college," she began thoughtfully, before pausing; "But it's… I don't live in Dublin. I from down the country, in the south," she finished.

"Not a factory girl." Luc continued to examine her intently.

"No, Mick the manager saw me paying one weekend in Kilkenny and asked me to come on this trip. I couldn't say no. A chance to play, travel and see Paris."

"And the nuns look after you well, yes?"

Both Helen and Angela nodded their approval in unison; "Of course. Couldn't be better."

"But maybe they are not so happy to see me here a man on this roof, the roof without a leak," he smiled once more.

"We won't spill the beans, if you don't," Angela suggested conspiratorially.

"And now my boss, he wonders where I am, and I must say *Au Revoir*."

Angela tapped the football; "And thanks for bringing our ball back.

Luc turned to leave, but as he did, he stopped himself; "You are both welcome. And will I see you again?"

Neither girl could have sworn to it, but it appeared this request might just have been directed at Helen.

"You can watch us play Saturday if you like," she answered eagerly.

"I would like that. And before Saturday?"

"You can if you like," Helen replied indifferently

"Jusqu'a la prochaine fois," Luc turned and made his way across the roof. The girl's gazes followed him. They watched him as stepped over the ledge onto the adjacent roof and rejoined his work colleagues.

"What do you think?" Helen asked giddily.

"Not my cup of tea," Angela answered dully. She tossed Helen the ball; "And you?"

"A bit, like yourself, Angela girl," Helen joked; "Easy on the eye!"

*

Sr. Monica loved the solitude of the roof at this time of the day. She went there every evening to pray, the faint singing of the sisters from the chapel her only backdrop. The day had been excessively hot, and now the refreshing higher air was a pleasant relief for her. She enjoyed this time to herself, but to-night was different. She felt a presence. She was not alone. She looked over her the shoulder just in time to see the young girl stop in her tracks. She was boyish in appearance, a purple band keeping her short hair off her forehead, but her sallow skin was flawless, t-shirt, shorts and plimsolls. As their eyes met, there was a look of complete mortification on the young girl's face.

"O God, I didn't realise, I'm so sorry, sister," the girl spluttered.

"Don't be."

"I didn't mean to intrude, I'll let you be." She sounded like she wished the ground would swallow her up.

"No don't go," Sr. Monica said reassuringly.

The young girl seemed wracked with indecision; "I should. The others will be wondering where I've got to," she answered apologetically.

"And are you enjoying your stay?"

"Brilliant."

"Good," Sr. Monica said encouragingly; "And the football?"

The question seemed to settle her.

"We drew a game and play again Saturday." She made another attempt to back away; "I'm really sorry for bothering you."

Sr. Monica beckoned the girl to join her; "No, please stay, sit awhile."

As the girl crossed timidly and sat beside her, they both took a moment to saviour the evening.

"It is nice here," the girl said thoughtfully.

"I think so. I like to come here during recreation hour. It is peaceful. I can think. Talk to God."

"I really should leave," the girl suggested awkwardly.

Sr. Monica shook her head gently; "Don't be silly. Please stay a while longer. It's not often we have visitors and from home too."

"I will so sister. I'm Helen, Helen Grace," she offered her hand.

"And call me Monica, please." The handshake was brief.

"Monica," Helen repeated the name to herself; "It is peaceful here, peaceful but…" she hesitated.

"Go on, child," Sr. Monica encouraged.

"I don't think I could live like this."

"And I'll let you in on a little secret, Helen. That was me once. The not knowing I could do it."

"And what changed?"

"Now I know I can."

Helen thought for a moment; "How can you be so sure?"

"Nobody is ever fully sure, are they? So, every evening I come up here and talk to God. He listens."

"And your family and friends?"

"The sisters are my family now. And yourself? Where are you from?"

"Bennettsbridge."

"Lovely. I grew up in Ross, Rosscarberry. My parents have a pub there, O'Donnell's. My brother runs it now. I spent many happy summers there.

"And did you ever play a bit of ball?"

"No. It was frowned upon."

Helen watched her closely as she spoke. In comparison to how she was coping to herself with the muggy heat, Sr. Monica seemed cool and serene. It was difficult to make out her features with the veil and white headdress which framed her head and seemed to constrain her upper body, but there wasn't a stray hair in sight. Although Helen could make out the beginning of some faint lines around her eyes and the corner of her mouth, she thought it impossible to put an age on her. The one unquestionable was that an ease had descended between them and Helen felt completely comfortable as Sr. Monica opened up even further, sharing with her how she had made a choice in her life, wanted God in her life and never wanted to forget his presence, leaving Ireland when she was; "ready, ready to learn and ready to help others." Helen listened attentively, barely interrupting as Sr. Monica detailed that it hadn't all been plain sailing and that she had relied on the power of prayer to make the right choices in the face of strident opposition from her father, who had tried to get her to; "see sense."

"You make it sound so easy," Helen mused.

"God lifts our prayers and makes them useful."

"I want to go to college in Dublin," Helen blurted in response and immediately felt embarrassed.

"Good for you," Sr. Monica nodded in agreement.

"I want a life. To meet new people, make new friends, meet boys, you know what I mean, "Helen attempted to explain further.

"I do."

"And did you ever want that?" Helen asked shyly.

"My life is busy thanking God, just in different ways."

"I want to be free to do what I want to do," Helen said with more conviction.

"And can you not do that at home?"

"No sister."

Sr. Monica grimaced briefly; "Monica, please, or Linda if you like. I haven't been called that for a while."

Helen considered what Sr. Monica had just told her, considered it as a sharing of sorts, an intimacy.

"Linda, why that's a beautiful name," she concluded.

"Sometimes I miss it. Monica is my Carthusian name. Linda O'Donnell, that's what the Ross crowd would know me by. Paddy and Bernie's young one who ran away to be a nun." She gave a hearty laugh.

"Ran off?"

"Stories get legs. They couldn't understand why I didn't want an eligible young farmer."

Sitting beside each other as they were, Helen could not help but notice Sr. Monica's porcelain-like skin, piercing blue eyes, angular cheekbones and jaw line. Her fingers were long and delicate and also appeared bloodless. In her mind's eye, Helen tried to marry this version of Sr. Monica with another image of her as a West Cork farmer's wife, Fair Isle jumper, oilskins tucked inside her wellies, yard brush in hand, cleaning down an outhouse steaming in hot cow shite.

"And was there ever a boy, an eligible farmer?" she asked brightly.

"Maybe one." Sr. Monica's tone was flat.

"And what became of him?"

"It was nothing. Short-lived. We kissed a few times. Held hands once."

"That doesn't sound like nothing to me," Helen said with certainty.

"It was to me."

"And did you ever?" Helen was shocked by the personal nature of her own question and tried to disguise that.

"Lord no. Nothing like that. It never made me feel I wanted to act."

"And him?"

"Told me one time that I made him feel wanted and that he wanted me."

Sr. Monica scanned the horizon and Helen tried to make sense of what Linda O'Donnell from Roscarrberry was laying out before her so coldly. She tried to reconcile it with her own absolute desire to want to be with a boy one day. As she listened further it became even more difficult for her to fathom, Sr. Monica's complete conviction that such a marriage was not how she wanted to be seen in the world and her unyielding belief that there was more purpose to her life here in France, having given herself to God and his mission for her. As their conversation unfolded, Helen had no doubt that Sr. Monica truly believed that she also had a freedom to do what she wanted in her life.

"And the eligible farmer?"

"I joined La Carthusian and never saw him again."

"And did you tell him how you felt?"

"No."

"I think you should have."

"And why do you think that?"

"For his sake, if nothing else."

"I didn't feel the need."

"And your father?"

"We lost contact."

That, above all everything else, Helen struggled with the most. She could never envisage that. Her mother had died young, and her father had never taken on another woman to replace her. It had always been just him and Helen, eking out a life in that small cottage at the edge of the village. Helen knew the locals talked of her mother's death as a shocking blow, but her passing was part of who herself and her father had become, and now there was the guilt of wanting to go to college and the worry of how he might cope alone. She had mentioned it to him in passing, but they had never sat down and fleshed out the detail of what Helen's actual moving to Dublin might entail, or the costs involved in such a move. She knew deep down that ultimately he would never stand in her way, and he would offer assurances that it would be what her mother would have wanted and that he himself would be bursting with pride for her. None of this eased her feelings of disquiet.

"I worry," Helen confided.

"Worries are only normal," Sr. Monica replied evenly: "God can help you with those."

"God is your answer to everything," Helen exclaimed in frustration and immediately regretted the outburst; "I'm sorry, Monica. I've no right to say that. You nuns have been nothing but good to us since we arrived," she corrected.

"Putting your trust in God for guidance isn't easy. There is a risk in really letting go."

"But turning your back on your family and friends," Helen shrugged in confusion; "It's not natural."

"It's not the first time that's been said," Sr. Monica answered cryptically.

"Your father?"

"Yes."

"Maybe if he could come out and visit, see for himself," Helen suggested.

"Maybe, but it's not encouraged."

"And the boy?"

"What about him?"

"Maybe you could help him to move on. Maybe that's all they both need, a gentle nudge."

"I'll keep that in mind if you do one thing for me."

"What's that sister?"

"To live the life God gave you."

"I'll try."

"Will you pray with me so, for both?"

Sr. Monica offered Helen her hand and she took it without compulsion. Sr. Monica then leaned forward in silent prayer, and Helen followed her lead. At that moment, it felt to Helen like the most natural thing in the world. In the distance, the chapel was quiet.

*

From her vantage point on the roof's balcony, she surveyed the chapel below. Angela was standing with her back to Helen, hands placed squarely on the ledge, allowing the cooler morning air caress her face. She could barely contain her bafflement.

"And that's all she had to say for herself, this Irish nun. That it was all God's plan."

"Yes," Helen answered sheepishly.

Angela turned to face Helen, resting her back against the ledge, "That's bonkers," she chuckled.

"She made it sound like the right thing to do for her."

"Praying and baking bread all day. How can that make sense?" Angela was unrelenting.

"You didn't meet her," Helen argued defiantly.

"Can we just talk about something else so?" Angela turned to face the chapel once more.

Helen did want to talk about something else, ever since the subject had been broached the previous day. She was bothered. She knew that Angela would never do anything intentionally to hurt Bob and Kit. Angela idolised her grandparents. They had after all taken her in and reared her as their own when Angela's father had gone to England, and it had all gotten too much for mother, but Helen was fearful that all this heady talk of a contract in France would cloud Angela's judgement. Angela needed to stay grounded, and this was Helen's opportunity.

"Professional football. How does that even work?"

"I'll know more tomorrow. Mick is bringing me to meet Pierre again."

"And when were you going to tell me this?" Helen asked accusingly.

"Amn't I telling you now," Angela cracked, turning angrily.

"And what is this meeting about?"

"Another chat."

"Just a chat?"

Angela threw her arms out in frustration; "Jesus, I don't know, Helen. If Saturday goes well. Who knows."

"And when are you going to tell them at home about this?"

"Soon." Angela turned away, disgruntled.

Helen left it lie. She had to tread carefully. Football was the only oulet that meant something to Angela. It brought her alive, the one aspect of her life where she could hold her head up and say look at me. Helen didn't want to push her away. She crossed to join her and placed one hand gently on her back; "So, what's the plan?"

"You really are a great person, Helen," Angela sighed, leaning her head into Helen's shoulder.

"What do you mean?"

Angela turned her head and fixed her eyes on Helen: "There's no backdoors with you. You tell it as it is."

"Thanks."

Helen could feel her throat tighten. She thought of her father and how growing up he had instilled that trait in her, and she remembered the night her mother died and how as a six-year-old girl she was brought to her mother's bedside. Her mother had taken Helen's hand in hers, Helen never forgetting the weakness of the grip, and looking up from her deathbed her mother had whispered; "Be an honest girl now for your mammy and pray for me." Her mother had held Helen's hand then briefly before allowing it to slip away.

Helen could feel herself welling up.

"Jesus, come here to me. I'm sorry for upsetting you." Angela embraced Helen.

"Look at the state of me." Helen's voice was a mixture of laughter and tears as she fought to compose herself.

"Here, let me." Angela took a hanky from her pocket and dabbed Helen's tears. The girls were looking at each other now, their faces within touching distance.

"And now you have started me off," Angela sobbed.

"What are we like, the pair of us," Helen laughed, holding back fresh tears.

"No, you are spot on, Helen. I need to do right. Be true to myself," Angela sniffled.

Helen threw her arms around Angela in a comforting hug; "It will work out fine, you'll see." before releasing her and leaving her hands on her shoulders.

"Let me tidy you up now," she offered, taking the hanky off Angela and wiping her face clean.

"How do I look?" Angela asked.

Helen took a step back to take stock; "You look, beautiful again."

"I just feel…I don't know what I feel," Angela faltered.

Helen placed the palm of her hand on Angela's breastbone; "Your heart is racing."

"It is, isn't it. It's so stupid." Angela cast her eyes down.

Helen took Angela's hand in her own and placed it on Angela's beating heart, holding it there soothingly.

"Feel that," Helen said quietly.

"I know, silly."

"Listen. It's so quiet up here," Helen murmured; "Can you feel it?"

With that, Angela leaned her forward and kissed Helen on the lips.

*

Helen needed to clear her head. She needed this time away from football, from her teammates, Mick and away from…

"And where is Angela today?" Luc asked casually. He was pacing the roof before her, taking in the views.

"She had to meet someone," Helen answered indifferently.

"Sounds, how do you say? Very mysterious."

"Well, I'm sure it's not."

"And Angela did not ask you to come with her to meet someone?"

"I had no interest."

"And Angela she was happy, no, to go alone."

"Why do you keep asking me about Angela?" Helen fired irritably; "I don't really care what she thinks. I told you I had no interest."

Luc stopped and made a gesture of surrender; "My pardon. Maybe you also want to be alone today." And he turned to leave.

"No, wait. Don't go. I'm sorry for snapping like that, "Helen answered guiltily; "I'd like you to stay, if you want to, that is."

"No, it is my fault. I should not poke my nose in other people's business."

"And I shouldn't be such a bitch," Helen acknowledged.

Luc crouched over her and signaled for permission to sit alongside; "May I?"

"Of course."

"*Je ne pense pas tu es un chienne,*" Luc said lightly as he took his place beside her.

"And what does that mean?" Helen frowned.

"It means I like you. Not a bitch. Ok."

The beginnings of a faint smile crept across Helen's face; "I can be sometimes," she admitted.

"And today is one of those days?"

"It might be," Helen added candidly;" You see myself and Angela, we had a…misunderstanding."

"Shh," Luc stopped her elaborating; "No more talk about Angela. We agreed."

"We did," Helen laughed, throwing her head back; "And that sun. It looks like you could pluck it right out of the sky."

"Lie back," Luc suggested eagerly.

"What?" Helen's face was awry with confusion.

"Trust me. Just lie back. We can do this together."

Helen reluctantly did as Luc asked and, beside her, he was doing likewise.

"Now reach out as far as you can and block the sun with the palm of your right hand."

Helen giggled, tilted her head towards him and followed his lead.

"Hold your palm there and relax. Very slowly now make a fist. Be careful, *peu a peu.* Close your eyes and when I count to three sit up gradually; "Don't drop it. Eyes closed, *un, deux, trois."*

"What are we like!" Helen joked, doing as he did.

They were both sitting upright now with their right hands clenched.

"Open your eyes, but don't drop it." Luc turned to face Helen and looked at her deeply: "I will give you mine first and keep it safely, yes. Show me your other hand."

Helen held out her left hand and as she did Luc cupped his right hand over it; "And now you nice and gentle."

Helen followed suit, her right hand to his left. As she did, their eyes met once more. His face was a blend of manliness and gentility. She felt lightheaded, her pulse quickening and her colour rising.

"We have exchanged a special gift now," Luc said earnestly; "The gift of sunlight. Keep it safe, where you can visit it anytime." He placed his left hand over his own heart. Helen smiled and touched the side of her head; "I will." Her eyes were sparkling.

"And now you smile, lovely again."

"So, maybe I won't be a bitch today after all."

"And to-night we will reach for the stars."

"Tonight?"

They drew back from each other.

"Yes, a proper date.," Luc nodded; "Me and you. It is ok, yes."

"Yes, I would like that," Helen smiled, reaching out and resting her hand on his.

*

Angela was alone. She was absolutely livid with herself. The one true friend she could confide in, share with. How could she have gotten the signals so badly wrong? All day, when she had thought about it, she had felt nauseated. And now there she was crossing the roof purposefully. Angela's face froze.

"I was wondering where I'd find you."

"I needed some place to think," Angela said broodingly.

"Can I stay?" Helen asked.

"If you want to." Angela looked away.

Helen sat beside her; "What do you think?" she asked willfully.

"Honestly," Angela swallowed and looked at Helen softly in the eyes; "I don't know. Are we ok, the two of us, after…yesterday?" Angela lowered her head.

"I'm here, aren't I?"

"Still friends so." There was a strain in Angela's voice, and she shifted uneasily where she sat. A smile widened across Helen's face.

"Of course we are you, silly goat. Now, to be fair, I didn't know you fancied me!" Helen said breezily.

"I don't," Angela exhaled.

Helen placed her arm around Angela's shoulder; "And as much as I love you…"

"Not like that," Angela finished the sentence for her.

"No."

"It's something between us now," Angela suggested circumspectly.

"And that's where it will stay."

Angela allowed herself to relax. Helen's assuagement confirmed for her what she always believed to be true that Helen was indeed a good decent person, a fearless person and as they sat side by side in comfortable silence Angela took the opportunity to divulge to this good friend that, she was finally coming to the realisation that she couldn't live this life of secrecy anymore, but that she needed more time to "work it through" and for once in her life "try and put herself first".

Growing up Angela had never felt any attraction for the boys in her neighbourhood. She had used them as a means to an end to improve herself as a football player, but her deeper desires she had kept suppressed. As a teenager, that had been difficult for her, the confusion. At first, it had appeared easier to live the lie, but that had meant that the world away from the football pitch had been a troubled and lonely place for her. These were the feelings she felt she could never reveal to Bob or kit, and that added to the melancholy of her young adulthood. There had been one brief, fleeting period of respite during her final year at school, a furtive relation-ship with an older girl. Angela had believed this girl when she had said nice things to her, believed she was telling the truth. And then the crushing blow when she told Angela that for her, it was just a bit of "messing around", "experimenting."

Angela looked at Helen. Her eyes were warm and filled with understanding.

"What happened after that?" Helen asked kindly.

"We stopped being close."

"Well, we won't," she said definitively.

"Thanks Helen. That means a lot to me."

Helen leaned towards Angela; "Now come on, tell me how that meeting went this morning?"

"They want me to sign, after the game tomorrow. What I always wanted," Angela answered drearily.

Helen clapped her hands with delight and thrust her-self forward; "That's brilliant news. You see things are looking up."

"Then why do I feel so miserable?"

"Because we are Irish. We are born that way." Helen jumped to her feet; "Let's celebrate." She crouched and began to haul Angela upright also.

"It's not straightforward," Angela said reticently, straightening herself; "They want me to start immediately."

"And what did you say?"

"That I'd think about it."

"And have you?"

"All my life."

"Well then."

Angela shrugged and walked to the roof edge.

"Whatever makes you less miserable," Helen cautioned.

"And back home?" Angela asked quietly, scanning the horizon.

"Talk it all through with them. Tell them everything. How you feel?"

Angela turned to face Helen. Her face was filled with doubt; "Everything?"

"Yes."

"No, Helen, I couldn't face that."

*

Some evenings, prayers came easier than others for Sr. Monica. She had felt a deep unquiet all day, and her acquired understanding of how God liked to test her from time to time did little to quell her apprehension. She knew that one passed these tests by being patient, by listening and by waiting. She had immersed herself in the Carthusian teachings; the importance of faith and the opening of one's mind and heart to allow the sign to come. She truly believed that the simplest thing in the world was to allow Jesus into her life, to make time for it, to follow it, believe it, and finally to put your life in the hands of the greater power. She had followed La Carthusian to a fault, yet tonight she could not shake the nagging doubts. Where once she thrived in its solitude, now she was glad to see the young vibrant Irish girl enter the roof space once more. She reminded her of herself in a different lifetime. Was this God's ultimate test for her?

Can I ask you something?" Helen enquired tentatively.

"Of course."

"A personal question."

"Go ahead."

Helen took a slow breath; "Do you miss her?"

"Who?" Sr. Monica looked puzzled.

"Linda."

"I have no regrets, if that's what you mean," Sr. Monica said calmly.

"None." Helen's tone was filled with surprise.

"Linda had no direction in her life."

Helen took a moment. She needed to get her head around Sr. Monica referring to herself in the third person. It was disconcerting for her; "But don't you ever wonder about that life?"

"Today, all day, I have been pre-occupied. Something you said yesterday," Sr. Monica answered thoughtfully.

"It wouldn't be the first time I put my foot in it."

"You asked me had I ever played football. That was something we would never even dream of doing, been allowed to even contemplate and now, this life, this is my choice. I don't expect you to understand that. Not in a weekend."

Helen was watching Sr. Monica's studiously, but her face was betraying no emotion.

"And then it got me thinking about Ross," she continued; "What was expected of me, Linda. I don't miss that. And I have thought about my father today, for the first time in a long time."

"Have you made a decision?" Helen interrupted.

"No."

"And the boy?"

"John, and he was just a boy. So, I have been thinking about this, and it's been troubling me all day that maybe I do miss her, but not her life. Can you understand that?"

"It makes perfect sense to me," Helen agreed.

"That I don't want to lose that part of myself."

"That's not a sin, is it? To want to be yourself."

Sr. Monica allowed herself a faint knowing smile; "The sisters say doubts are sent to challenge us. To make us stronger."

"Your father, this boy John, they are part of who you are not doubts."

"What are you saying?"

"Not to forget that."

"Sometimes Linda can make life difficult for me," Sr. Monica admitted, joining her hands.

"Maybe, she just needs to stop running."

"I hope you get what you want, Helen, you truly deserve it." Sr. Monica then raised her right arm and offered Helen a blessing.

"I'll find a way. I always do."

"Promise me that."

"If you do one thing for me."

"If I can."

"Those days Linda O'Donnell from Rosscarberry is making life hard for you, you need to make peace with her. Will you do that for me?"

"Deal."

They exchanged a brief hug and as Sr. Monica watched Helen leave, she felt comforted. This young Irish girl had spoken openly, honestly and bravely. Sr. Monica moved to the balconies edge and looked out at the reddening night sky. She knew it was thought inappropriate in the public areas, but she couldn't resist the overwhelming urge. She slowly and meticulously unclipped her veil, removed her *bandeau* and shook her hair free and for one daring moment she was Linda O'-Donnell once more.

*

Helen and Luc were both lying facing skywards, hand in hand. Helen had never seen anything quite like this indigo sky mottled in every direction as far as the eye could see with clear stars. Earlier in the evening had been equally impressive. While the team had gone to an Irish bar in the *18th Arrondissement* to celebrate their victory, Luc had taken Helen to see Paris in all its glory.

The sights, sounds, and smells of the city had fascinated her, and she felt practically drunk from the exuberance of it all.

What had been most striking had been the riot of colour at each site; The Arc de Triomphe, The Eiffel Tower, a far cry from the staid black and white images she had been exposed to in her school books. Before her very eyes, these monochrome images of her mind's eye exploded into living, breathing places. The sounds of the city equally enthralled her, the honking of car horns, the chatter of French accents, and she had stepped endearingly around the footpath grilles that allowed blasts of hot air to escape as the metro's trundled below.

The conversation had flowed naturally between them, and Luc had told her of his upbringing in Crisenoy, a small village outside of Paris. He spoke openly about how in the beginning he had found life at the Sorbonne difficult. He had been torn by loneliness when he arrived first, conflicted by the pull of Crisenoy, the place his ambition was always to leave. Initially, all he wanted to do was go back there, but he explained how eventually these feelings passed and now being away from home and loved ones felt perfectly normal.

Helen felt comfortable in his presence and shared her worries about leaving her father to pursue her own dreams. Luc reassured her that it was alright to feel these emotions, but that everybodys life must change. "You will love it;" he had enthused; "And your father will be happy because you are happy." Helen hadn't wanted the evening to end, and she knew she would remember it for the rest of her life, remember this night, no matter how many times she would return to Paris, and she was determined to return one day. And so, they had found themselves back on the roof where they first met only a few days previously.

"What are you thinking?" Helen asked shyly.

"That this is very beautiful, and you?"

"That we are very small."

"*Petite.*"

"Two tiny dots."

"*Deux petits points.*"

"And the stars?"

"*L'etoiles.*"

"Doesn't the whole world seem, very…fragile," Helen pondered.

"The Gods are very happy tonight. The stars create life. What is within the stars is life itself."

Helen gave a little laugh, sat forward and released his hand; "Do you believe that?"

"Of course."

"What do you see in the stars?" she asked, looking across at him with curiosity.

"That your eyes are…" Luc's voice faded.

"What about them?"

"They are…Can I kiss you?"

"You don't need to ask."

"But the kiss is the most precious of all. It must never be stolen," Luc said sitting up beside her.

"Our manger tried to kiss me once."

"What happened?"

"I brushed him off."

Luc leaned towards her and his fingers brushed her cheek as he pushed her hair back from her face. He cupped his hands and eased her towards him; "Do you want to brush me off?" he smiled gently. Their lips were touching softly now.

"No," Helen sighed in breathless anticipation as she felt the warmth of his touch under her blouse.

*

The two girls had come to squeeze as much time out of the glorious weather as they could muster. Helen had her arms out by her side to prop herself up. Her eyes were closed, and she had her face pointing directly in the line of fire of the sun. She could feel her forehead, face and breastbone getting hot, but she didn't care anymore. Beside her, Angela was engrossed in the morning newspaper Mick had brought back from the village. She was using her thumb and index finger to snap through the pages mercilessly.

"It was everything I thought it would be," Helen said confidentially, but the only reply was the sound of page slapping on page.

"Are you even listening to me?" Helen turned to Angela, her voice filled with aggravation.

"I am. It was everything you thought it would be," Angela recited back without lifting her head.

"What?" Helen challenged.

"Paris," Angela answered, finally looking up and raising her eyebrows.

"My point exactly. You haven't been listening to a word I've been saying. Me and Luc."

"You need to be careful with those French lads. They only want one thing from a girl," Angela warned.

"And Mick?"

"Mick has done a lot for me."

"He is still a slim-ball though," Helen retorted.

"He is," Angela agreed; "Now take a look at that." Angela smoothed the newspaper out across her thighs with the palm of her hand.

"What am I looking for?"

"See do you recognise anyone," Angela replied, brandishing a smile.

Helen didn't need to look twice. There she was in black and white, in all her glory, Angela. She was balancing balletically on her right foot, body arched in unison and her face a study in concentration. She was about to shift the ball beyond her French opponent with her left foot and cut back inside. The French girl had the pained look of defeat on her face, the dawning realisation that in an instant Angela would be gone, leaving her in her wake. She was flailing hopelessly, trying to catch hold of Angela's right cuff.

"Sweetest Jesus!" Helen proclaimed; "That's you and that's the goal."

"I'm famous," Angela smiled proudly.

Helen peered closely at the caption beneath the photograph:

Cette femme est dangereuse.

"They think I'm dangerous!" Angela emphasised wildly.

"Brilliant!" Helen threw her head back freely, clapping her hands.

Angela began to fold the newspaper, and she handed it to Helen: "Will you show it to Bob and Kit when you get back?"

"And can't you do that? Helen asked, holding the paper out from her body awkwardly.

"I wish you had come back to the bar with us, Helen. We had a glass of champagne to celebrate, and they are going to pay me twenty French pounds a week." Angela's eyes were sparkling with exhilaration; "And I need you to do that massive favour for me."

"This." Helen gave the paper a slight wave and scrunched her face up in unsureness.

"Yes."

"I don't understand." Helen sounded bewildered.

"They want me to start straightaway. Three games in Italy next month, pre-season."

At first, Helen's bafflement deepened, the blur of how Angela did not intend travelling home to Ireland in the morning instead embarking on her new life for herself and imposing on Helen to smooth this decision over with her grandparents, just to tide Angela over until things settled down, but Helen quickly gathered herself.

"Not a hope," Helen said staunchly.

"But I can make a life here, the life I want to live, the way I want to live it."

"I can't do this," Helen pleaded, her voice shaking with every word.

"I promise I will explain everything the first chance I get."

"Everything."

"Yes."

"Promise."

Angela blessed herself resolutely; "I give you, my word. I can get home for Christmas."

"Christmas," Helen enunciated.

"I wouldn't ask you, but I need someone I can trust."

Helen made to hand back the newspaper to Angela.

"Can you do this for me, please? I'm begging you."

"You better look after yourself," Helen said, taking the newspaper back and setting it down beside her; "And score some goals."

The girls exchanged a long hug and in the intensity of the moment didn't realise they were no longer without company.

"*Bonjour mes demoiselles.*" Luc's greeting was in keeping with the brightness of the day; "I came to say *au revoir* to you both, and I brought a gift for everyone." He was carrying a brown bag close to his chest.

Angela shifted to one side and made room for Luc to sit between them: "Squeeze in there, so nice and cosy!"

Luc sat between them, placing the bag between his legs.

"And Angela has news Luc. She is staying here in France to play football."

"*Fantastique!* We can drink to that." Luc took three bottles from the bag."

"What's that?" Helen asked.

"Coca," Luca replied, handing her one of the bottles. She took the bottle gingerly and ran her hand over its curved shape; "I've never seen it."

"Boisson non alcoolise, a soda," Luc explained as he handed Angela a bottle; "Do you think you will spend many years in professional football, Angela?"

"I hope so," Angela said as both herself and Helen held their bottles up for closer inspection.

"Please allow me," Luc said, and he produced a *Swiss Army Knife* from his pocket and systematically began opening the bottles with the corkscrew, first Helen, then Angela and finally himself. He raised his own bottle theatrically, then; *"Sante!* to Angela, her football, *l'avenir."* They clinked their glasses then before drinking in silence.

Angela was the first to speak; "Pretty good." She then held the bottle up towards the sun again.

"Helen? *C'est delicieux,* tastes good, no," Luc asked approvingly.

"Sweet."

"Bon gout."

"That's it…bon gout," Helen repeated.

*

Helen had never gone that far with a boy before, and she was glad it had been with Luc. She had nearly been overwhelmed as her body convulsed under the lightness of his touch down there before she took his arousal in her hand. At first, he had placed his hand over hers and guided the slow rhythmic movement before trusting her to finish. She was pleased that he had surrendered himself in this way to the sensitivity of her touch and at the moment of climax she also had felt a frisson of energy course through her own body as his body shuddered, and his face contorted in ecstasy. And then she held him tenderly as he emptied himself fully and his breathing became shallower. At that moment, she was taken by the heat of him, and then he slumped into her arms. It had been an awakening for her, and she knew that on returning home, the feeble fumbling of the lads down the rugby club would never be enough to satisfy her. She had basked in the intimate warmth of it all day, but now the inevitability of a parting hung between them.

"Will I see you again?" Luc asked Helen, fixing her an inquisitive look.

"When you come to Ireland."

"And that makes me a little sad."

"You must go back to college and I must…I know what I want now. Anything else wouldn't be fair on either of us."

"I want to show you something," Luc said, taking Helen by the hand.

"Where?"

"Something special." Luc led Helen across the roof to the balcony ledge and pointed into the middle-distance; "Look, just there," he advised, shifting Helen's body lightly in the direction he was pointing; "There, through the trees…*la tourelle, a gauche.* That roof, *la rose,* the pink one."

There in the glare of the sun, Helen could make out a pink domed building, its green roof tiles glistening in the sun.

"Yes, I can see it."

"*Chateau Marianne,*" Luc said dramatically.

"It is very beautiful."

"*La famille Duplessis* had it built for their daughter Marianne and her lover Jean when he left to fight the British at Gibraltar. It was a famous battle." Luc's voice was soft, controlled.

"The Brits are always fighting someone." Helen screwed her face up in disgust.

"Built as a symbol of their love to each other." Luc placed his left arm on Helen's shoulder and leaned across her with his right hand pointing forward; "If you look closely, you can see the J and M, the initials of the two lovers on that roof there." Helen took her guide from Luc and strained her eyes; "Yes, I can make that out."

Luc stooped forward slightly; "And now look below, the two hands joined as a symbol of fidelity."

"I see them."

"And now I will make a memory for both of us that will not evaporate." Luc straightened himself. The Swiss Army Knife was out again, and he began etching on the wooden handrail.

"What are you doing? Helen recoiled in shock.

"Wait and see." Luc was concentrating fully on the handrail, moving along it slowly working the knife in his right hand, and clearing away the shavings into the summer air with his left; "In France we say nothing can separate those who love each other, not even time."

"Jesus, stop! The nuns will blow a gasket!"

Luc continued, head bent, finished the carving and wiped it with his sleeve before standing back proudly; "And now nothing can come between us, look." He closed the knife shut and returned it to his pocket. Helen stepped forward and ran her finger along the fresh carving:

L & H

Trentiemme du Julliet, dix-neuf soixante-douze

She turned her head to Luc; "And what happened the two lovers?"

"He never returned. Marianne lived a long life with many husbands, but Jean was always her true love."

Helen read the inscription aloud; "L and H, July thirtieth, nineteen seventy-two."

"You're last day in France."

"No doom and gloom, not today. Say something in French, something nice, something we will remember."

"Aujourd'hui est le premier jour du reste de nos vies...I said…"

But before Luc could explain, Helen had placed her hand on his lips; "Shh stop. I don't need to know. Just hold me one more time like before."

*

Sr. Monica was exactly where Helen had expected to find her. Helen wanted to thank her for the hospitality, but also needed to tell her that her mind was settled, and she was determined to set the train in motion on arrival back in Bennettsbridge. She would sit her father down and have a proper heart-to-heart. They could work something out.

"Our prayers were answered so," Sr. Monica smiled benignly.

"They were weren't they."

"And I learned some things about myself," she confided.

"What kind of things?" Helen looked surprised.

"That I wasn't happy and a bit lost. I listened to what you had to say," Sr. Monica said with a half-smile.

"Me?"

"Yes, the Lord moves in mysterious ways. I feel that I can breathe now, that a great weight has been lifted.

"That's nice to hear."

The two women stood as a pleasant evening air rolled in, neither of them speaking.

Sr. Monica eventually broke this peaceful hush; "Can I show you something?" she asked politely.

"Of course you can."

"A little secret of mine. You mustn't tell."

"I wouldn't dream of it."

Sr. Monica took a piece of white linen from deep inside her habit. She unfolded it with great care and lay it on the palm of her hand for Helen to view; "You can take if you want."

Helen took the fabric cautiously and examined it; "A lock of hair," she said in wonderment.

"Mine, I've kept it against their will."

"Why?"

"At La Carthusian, they cut off our hair for Jesus. Sometimes I take it out to remind me of who I was."

Helen returned the linen to Sr. Monica gingerly and watched her as she refolded it with affection and replaced it inside her habit.

"A childish idea, I know," Sr. Monica said distantly.

"I don't think so."

"Can you do something else for me?"

"Anything at all, just ask."

With that, Sr. Monica took two envelopes from her habit and held one out for Helen; "Can you get this to my father?"

"Certainly."

"It explains everything, like you said."

"I'm so glad," Helen said, taking the envelope; "It will make you feel a whole lot better," she added genuinely.

"I do."

"And do you want me to say anything else?"

"That I am looking forward to seeing him, soon."

Sr. Monica then handed the second envelope to Helen; "And this is for John."

"I won't let you down," Helen said optimistically.

"That gentle nudge to help him move on." Sr. Monica said quietly.

"Is that all?"

"Yes, it's all in there."

"And I have a little secret," Helen revealed as she put the two envelopes away for safe keeping; "I met a boy."

"The French lad working on the roof," Sr. Monica declared.

Helen was taken aback; "You know."

"We sisters have our ways," Sr. Monica explained brightly with a sweep of her hands

"And we were together, last night."

"And how do you feel about that, today?" Sr. Monica asked, her tone was non-judgemental.

"Good, guilty…I dunno." Helen shrugged.

"Do you love this boy?"

"Not love. Is that a mortal sin, sister?"

"When I arrived here first my mother asked *La Mere Superieure* that if I ran away would it be a mortal sin."

"What did she say?"

"She told my mother that she could ask Jesus that herself when she met him."

"But what does that mean? Helen continued her face filled with bemusement. Sr. Monica paused to gather her thoughts before answering.

"For me, not to spend your life worrying and wondering," she offered eventually.

"Go with the flow."

"Living your life, child. May I give you one final blessing?"

"Yes, if you think it will do some good."

"It won't do any harm."

Helen bowed her head before Sr. Monica allowing her to place both her palms gently on Helen. Helen stood motionless as she received the silent blessing. Sr. Monica stepped back then and made a sign of the cross. The two women embraced spontaneously.

"I will deliver those letters for you," Helen said as they drew back from each other.

"Thank you."

"I'm glad I met you, Linda."

"The girl who ran away to be a nun!" Sr. Monica quipped.

Helen gave a jaunty wave and strolled casually across the rooftop for one final time. As Sr. Monica returned the wave, she felt content that her faith in the power of prayer and its ability to help people had been renewed. She was prepared to rededicate herself to that calling with even more fervour in the coming weeks and months ahead because that worked best when you accepted who you were yourself first. She was comfortable in her own skin again.

She crossed to the handrail and there she read the fresh hand carving. When she had finished reading, she removed the linen from her pocket one more time. She unfolded it slowly and then shook the strands of hair free into the summer night. Watching them being swept away in the wind, she crumpled up the lined fabric and thrust it back into the pocket of her habit. She rested her palms on the handrail once more with her head bowed:

L&H

Trentiemme du Julliet, dix-neuf soixante-douze
She knelt in prayer.

shapes that don't belong

Adelaide Prentiss[*]

Through twisted spires the path begins to wind,
Where mist hangs low like breath in brittle air.
The mountains speak in murmurs, long and slow,
A tongue unknown to those who climb too fast.

Each step a fractured beat, a pulse of stone,
The earth beneath my feet shifts in its sleep,
And every echo trembles in the void.

The sky above is bruised in hues of dusk,
A palette strange, with clouds that twist and break.
The light is thin, a gossamer of gold,
Yet tinged with something raw, a fractured glow.

I tread between the shadows' long descent,
Their fingers cold as they ensnare the rocks,
While somewhere far below the silence hums.

---

[*]Adelaide Prentiss is a college student from Florida studying
English Literature. She writes poetry and short stories, and is
an teaching assistant for the English Department. This is her
first published piece.

No trees here rise, but skeletal remains
Of trunks long withered by the mountain's breath.
Their limbs reach out like prayers that never end,
Bent toward a sky that holds no sympathy.

I brush their bark, its texture rough and worn,
It crumbles at the touch like dust or bone,
A memory of what the wind devours.

The path now veers, the stones grow sharp and thin,
Their jagged edges gleam like shards of glass.
I feel the mountain breathing through the gaps,
Its rhythm slow, yet deeper than the dark.

Each crevice yawns with secrets long entombed,
As if the earth had swallowed time itself,
And left these bones to weather in its sleep.
A raven wheels above, a shadowed blur,
Its cry cuts through the air like splintered ice.

It circles once, then vanishes from sight,
A sign, perhaps, of what the lake conceals.
I press ahead, my breath a measured rasp,
The altitude weighs heavy on my chest,
Yet still, the lake calls softly from beyond.

Through crooked passes, narrow as a breath,
I slide between the stones that scrape the sky.
The cliffs above lean in, as if to speak,

"shapes that don't belong"

But hold their silence, cold and coiled tight.

The air grows thick, a substance strange to touch,
It curls around my limbs, a serpent's coil,
And pulls me ever closer to the lake.

Now from the ridge I glimpse the water's edge,
A silver sliver nestled in the stone.
It gleams with light that does not come from stars,
But from some hidden source beneath the waves.

Its surface smooth, unbroken, still as glass,
Yet something stirs beneath its perfect skin,
A pulse that ripples faintly through the air.

I descend slow, the path no longer clear,
But etched by feet that tread in other times.
The ground gives way, the rocks a shifting skin,
And in the distance, silence holds its breath.

The lake awaits, a mirror cold and deep,
Its stillness strange, untouched by wind or storm,
A mystery untouched by waking eyes.
At last, I stand before its quiet form,
The water darker now, as night ascends.

It whispers soft, a sound like distant bells,
But warped, as though the echoes bent through time.
I kneel beside its edge, my hand extends,
But hesitate before the surface breaks,
For what I touch might never let me go.

I dip my fingers in, the chill is sharp,
A bite that travels quick through bone and blood.
The water stirs, a ripple spreads its wings,
And in its wake, I see what lies beneath.

The stars themselves are tangled in the depths,
But twisted, bent in shapes that don't belong,
A sky reflected wrong in every line.
I feel the pull, the water calls me near,
It hums with something old, a song of stone.

The wind has ceased, the world holds tight its breath,
As if the lake has swallowed even time.
I close my eyes, the night begins to fold,
And in the silence, something stirs below—
A shadow moves within the depths unseen.

The stars above now mirror those below,
But neither seems to tell the truth they hold.
I rise to leave, yet feel the lake remains,
Its presence vast, though silent in the dark.

The mountains, too, seem watchful as I climb,
Their shapes both known and strange against the sky,
As if they shift when no one's there to see.
With every step, the silence grows more thick,
A weight that presses close upon my chest.

The lake recedes, though still it hums beneath,

A presence felt but never truly known.
And as I leave the mountains in my wake,
I know their secrets linger in the air,
A world that bends and shifts when shadows fall.

The World Grows Wild

Red Semiakina *

Lost in the jungle, the world grows wild,
I tread through shadows, my steps beguiled.
The trees tower high with their leaves entwined,
Their roots like fingers that search and bind.

The sky, once blue, is hidden away,
By a canopy thick as the close of day.
The birds call out in cries unknown,
And I wander this world all alone.

The ground beneath, damp with decay,
Fades into whispers that lead me astray.
With water in hand, my only guide,
I walk through the silence, my fear amplified.

The sun's soft light is lost in the green,
A world untouched, both fierce and serene.

---

*Red Semiakina is a creative writer and painter. She lives in the
Mojave Desert area of California, raising her own food and
caring for animals. This is her third published poem.

The vines grip tight to every limb,
Each path more foreign, each shadow grim.

The jungle breathes with a heavy sigh,
Its pulse in the wind, its gaze in the sky.
I drink from my flask, the water cool,
But feel no comfort in this endless spool.
The hours stretch as the jungle hums,
A world alive with forgotten drums.

The echoes rise from the ancient ground,
Where no clear tracks or roads are found.
Each step, a venture into the thick,
Where nature's rules are strange and quick.

The beasts that stir beyond my sight,
Move like ghosts in the dimming light.
I feel the thirst grow deep within,
But ration the water, thin and thin.

Each sip a moment of fleeting grace,
As I journey deeper into this place.
The jungle whispers secrets old,
In languages only the trees have told.
I listen, but know not what they say,
Their voices lead me further astray.

The river's sound, faint in the air,
Is a promise of hope, but I know not where.
I follow its call, though it twists and winds,
Through labyrinths, only the jungle designs.

My breath grows shallow, my pace now slow,
The endless green has nowhere to go.
Around me the leaves shimmer and sway,
But offer no path, no clear way.

With water dwindling, I count each drop,
A quiet prayer for the thirst to stop.
But the jungle's heat bears down on me,
A weight of life that won't set me free.

Through ferns and branches, I stumble wide,
As the jungle swells, a living tide.
Each branch a barrier, each vine a snare,
But still I move, though I know not where.

The day bleeds out in hues of red,
The sun now sinking, the sky half-dead.
Night whispers close, its fingers cold,
And the jungle, in darkness, grows bold.

The stars above, hidden from sight,
Leave me alone in the heart of night.
I strain for sounds, for signs of life,
But find only the jungle's eternal strife.

My water's low, but still I drink,
Each swallow slow, each breath in sync.
It cools my throat, but not my soul,
As the fear within takes its toll.

The night is thick, the air stands still,
A heavy weight, a silent thrill.
I hear the creatures prowl and roam,
But I am lost, without a home.

The water, once a lifeline true,
Is now a memory I hold on to.
Its final drops, a fleeting grace,
As I stare into this endless space.

The jungle wraps me in its grip,
A wild embrace from which I slip.
I walk through the night, my footsteps slow,
With no clear path, no place to go.

The dawn will come, but I may not see,
For the jungle keeps its hold on me.
And as I fade into the green,
I wonder if I've ever been seen.

The water's gone, my strength grows thin,
But still I fight the pull within.
For though I'm lost, I won't give in,
To the jungle's call, its endless spin.

I press ahead through vine and tree,
Hoping that somewhere, I'll break free.
But the jungle, vast, won't let me go,
It's in my blood, it's all I know.

And as I take my final stride,
I leave no trace, just time to bide.
For in the jungle, lost I'll stay,
Until the green has worn away.

Between the Lines

T.J. Thompson [*]

Lena's phone buzzed softly on the nightstand, filling the quiet room with a gentle hum. Instinctively, she reached for it, her heart skipping a beat as she saw Adam's name on the screen. The text read:

"Are you awake?"

It was a simple question, yet it held immense significance between them. Lena glanced at the clock—2:13 AM. Her fingers hovered over the keys, a familiar pattern that had played out countless times before.

"Yeah. Couldn't sleep. You?" she typed and sent, knowing he was likely in the same state.

Adam's reply came almost instantly.

"Same. Been thinking about you."

Lena sighed, staring at the screen. This had been their way for almost a year now—text messages, constant and fleeting, yet the only thread connecting them. They hadn't spoken on the phone in months, hadn't seen each

---

*TJ Thompson is a high school teacher and basketball coach from Iowa. He teaches English, writes for the local paper, and is currently working on his first novel.

other in even longer. What had started as a temporary solution had stretched on, becoming the only way they could reach each other.

She tapped her phone nervously, yearning to express something profound, yet hesitant about the depth a mere message could truly convey. After much contemplation, she finally settled on a message:

"I miss you."

A long pause ensued, making her wonder if he had fallen asleep. When his response finally came, it was a simple yet profound statement: "I miss you too. Every day."

The words struck her heart, tightening her chest. She could almost visualize him, lying in his small apartment miles away, staring at his phone just as she was. Both of them felt the tug of their connection and the overwhelming sense of impossibility of being together. They had once joked about how their relationship was temporary, how they would soon bridge the distance between them. But as the months passed, life's complexities—work, family, and obligations—had a way of pulling them further apart. Now, their connection was reduced to these fragile digital words.

"When are we going to fix this?" Lena typed, her question lingering in the open space between them.

The dots on the screen blinked, indicating that he was typing back, but they kept disappearing. Her heart raced as she waited, wondering what he was trying to convey.

Finally, his message appeared.

"I don't know. I want to, but I don't know how. It feels like we're trapped in different worlds."

His words hit her harder than she had anticipated. She had been holding on to hope that something would change, that they would find a way to break free from the constraints that kept them apart. But Adam's text felt like an admission of defeat.

"I feel that too," she replied. *"But I don't want to lose us."*

She pressed send, the vulnerability in her words making her stomach churn. Her fingers hovered over the phone, waiting for his response, her mind racing. It was true—she didn't want to lose him, but how long could they keep going like this?

Her phone buzzed again.

"We won't. I promise."

The simplicity of his reply calmed her slightly. Adam had always been the anchor between them, the one who held on to certainty when she started to drift. But there was an aching emptiness in the promise. Promises were easy to type; it was the living that was hard.

Lena lay back on her bed, holding the phone to her chest as if it could somehow transfer the warmth of his words into something more tangible. She closed her eyes, trying to imagine him next to her, the feel of his arms around her, the sound of his breath. But imagination only went so far. She needed more than words on a screen.

When they first met, everything was effortless. They spent countless hours together, talking, laughing, and touching—things that now felt so distant. However, his job had taken him further away, while her obligations kept her grounded. They had promised to stay in touch, to let the distance not hinder their connection. But the distance had transcended physical boundaries. It had seeped into their conversations and the gaps between their texts.

She typed again.

"What if we met halfway? Right now. I'll drive."

"I wish I could. I genuinely do. But tomorrow's chaotic. But soon, I promise."

"Soon" had become a catch-all phrase for all the times they couldn't be together.

Lena's response was prompt.

"I hate soon."

*

The subsequent few days passed in a whirlwind of texts. They maintained a lighthearted tone, discussing work, exchanging amusing memes, and engaging in trivial conversations about their everyday lives. However, beneath the surface, an unspoken tension lingered, a chasm that no amount of messaging could bridge.

Lena had grown accustomed to staring at her phone for extended periods, eagerly awaiting his name to appear, hoping for some indication that things were about to change. Yet, every conversation felt repetitive, trapped in a loop they couldn't break free from.

One evening, after a long and exhausting day at work, Lena returned home and collapsed onto her couch. Her phone buzzed in her hand, and she saw Adam's name on the screen once more.

"How was your day?"

She stared at the message, experiencing a peculiar blend of frustration and sadness. How was her day? It was the same as every other day. She yearned for him, desired more, and felt ensnared in a relationship that only existed in the realm of pixels.

Before she could prevent herself, she typed:

"I can't do this anymore."

The moment she sent the message, her heart sank. What had she done? Panic surged through her as she stared at the screen, anxiously awaiting his response.

After what seemed like an eternity, the reply arrived.

"What do you mean?"

Lena's hands shook as she typed, struggling to find the right words. How could she explain her feelings without causing him pain? But she knew she couldn't continue pretending everything was okay.

"I just... I need more than this. More than texts and promises that never come true."

There was a long pause before Adam replied.

"I know. I'm sorry."

Lena swallowed hard, her heart aching at the simplicity of his words. She had expected more—a fight, an explanation, something. But all she got was an apology.

She typed again.

"I don't want to lose you, but I sense that we're already drifting apart."

The dots on the screen flickered, vanished, and reappeared as Adam typed and retyped his response. Finally, his message arrived.

"I've been feeling the same. I just couldn't find the right words."

Lena's breath caught in her throat. She hadn't anticipated him to confess it. She hadn't expected the vulnerability from him, the same vulnerability she'd been harboring for so long.

"So, what should we do next?" she typed, her hands trembling.

This time, the pause was even more prolonged. Lena stared at the screen, waiting, her heart pounding in her chest. She could sense the weight of the conversation, the weight of what they were both trying to express but couldn't fully articulate.

Finally, Adam's response appeared.

"I believe we need to cease pretending that this is sufficient."

Lena's heart sank. She had known this moment was coming, but seeing the words on the screen made it real. Tears welled in her eyes as she typed back.

"Are you saying we should end it?"

The reply arrived swiftly.

"I don't want to end this, but I'm at a loss for how to fix it. I can't seem to be with you the way we used to be."

Lena wiped away her tears, gazing at the message. She had always held on to the belief that they could find a way to make it work, that if they persisted, they could overcome any obstacle. But perhaps Adam was right. Maybe the physical distance between them had grown into something insurmountable.

She typed slowly, each word feeling like a final goodbye.

"Perhaps we should take a step back and figure out what we truly desire."

The dots on the screen reappeared, and then Adam's message came through.

"Perhaps you're correct. I detest this decision, but I can't deny that you might be right."

Lena closed her eyes, tears streaming down her face. She had never wanted it to end like this—not through text, not in the middle of the night. But maybe it was the only way.

"I love you, Adam," she typed, her heart breaking as she sent the message.

His reply was almost immediate.

"I love you too, Lena. Always."

And then, an eerie silence descended upon the room.

Lena fixed gazes on the screen, yearning for something more, but the screen remained unyielding. The conversation had abruptly concluded, leaving behind only the words, frozen in time, serving as a poignant reminder of what they had once shared.

Zapatos

Sylvia G Vega[*]

Zapatos. "I won't wear them!" My sister squirmed on the edge of the chair as our father, in his thick Cuban accent, handed the sample shoe to the Macy's salesgirl in the high heel patents.

"Mijita," he said in a whisper that was a disguised yell, "my daughter, these are sturdy, and will last you through the winter. And the laces--they will hold your feet firmly in place." He paused, smiling as the girl with the rosy cheeks and pretty legs reappeared, box in hand.

My mother--where *was* my mother? A department away, browsing through the *Barely There* stockings.

The salesgirl smiled, removing the lid from the box and tissue paper from inside the shoes. I admired her golden name tag; her name was Betsy, like my class-

[*]Sylvia Vega holds a B.A. in English from Northwestern University and an M.A. in English Literature from Arizona State University. She has taught third grade to college, sharing her passion for reading, writing, and storytelling. A proud mother of two sons pursuing their dreams in New York City and Los Angeles, Sylvia presented her project on the benefits of writing, titled "GPS: Navigating Your Life through Journaling," and is currently expanding it into a book.

mate. They *were* sturdy, this pair. Black clunky leather *zapatos* that looked like army boots. On the playground, when a kid got angry at me for getting to the tetherball first, he'd growled, "Your mother wears army boots." A first-grader having just begun to speak English a year ago, I had thought that was a funny thing to say. Now the image had materialized before me, and I understood the insult. My sister was right; they did look like *zapatos de miliciano,* army boots.

My sister was eleven, I was six. We were a newly arrived immigrant family in Astoria, Long Island, out of our element like tropical fish thrown into the Hudson. I see my parents differently now, the way we see more clearly when we discover that old photograph, and for the first time take in the expressions on the faces of our loved ones.

"No me los voy a poner!" Tears streaming down her face, my sister shot a look at Betsy, hoping to find sympathy, but another customer had stolen her away. "I won't wear them!" she snapped. "Why not those penny loafers, just like my old ones? I love those!"

"Mijita. Daughter…" There was that barely audible rage—behind the gentle smile and the even tone, a measured control that threatened to explode, like a crack in a dam about to break. "Those are just like your old ones, the ones that didn't last very long. And your feet, even with thick wool socks, slide out easily. I've watched you at the dinner table, your legs moving back and forth, your feet sliding those shoes on and off, on and off."

My father didn't do well with movement, across the ocean or beneath the table, it disturbed a stillness that, to his utter frustration, he constantly demanded from life.

His face became distorted. It did not redden, but stiffened, like cement hardening. Pausing to remove his glasses, the ones with the unbreakable frames, he delivered the final blow: "These are the right *zapatos.*"

I moved away, my attention drawn to a lovely pair of dress shoes: red patent leather with a strap and a bow, the shoes of my dreams. If only I could just try them on, I thought, and play in them for a little while, I could be a different little girl, like Mary Beth down the block, who takes ballet in a ruffly pink tutu, has Play-Doh in all four colors, and *familia* who giggle and hug.

Before we headed home, we stopped for a little while at Central Park. I skipped by the *Alice in Wonderland* statue, and I headed for the lush grass. My father bought Cracker Jacks, and I ate the whole box, minus the peanuts.

My mother--clutching the bag with the *zapatos*—and father sat on the park bench, enough space between them for two people. My sister sat on the knoll, her knees pulled up, so that she wrapped her arms around them and buried her face, her shiny black hair gleaming in the sun.

On the crowded subway ride home, the shopping bag sat on my mother's lap, while my father stood, a firm grip on the pole for balance. My sister didn't say a word, playing with her blue headband. I stared at my prize, a Sailor Jack badge, and couldn't stop thinking of a brightly colored ball some girls had at the park, the kind I often saw in a bin at the grocery store. I wanted to suck my thumb so badly, something I could get away with at home, but instead I tucked my badge in my pocket and my hands under my thighs.

When we arrived home, a one-bedroom apartment where the living room doubled as dining room and our bedroom, the *zapatos* lay on the couch for a moment until my father went to the bathroom, and my sister swiftly transported the box to beneath our parents' bed where she hoped they would remain hidden.

And except for one dreadful morning when my mother took an inordinate amount of time stirring the oatmeal, when there was yelling and tears and knots in shoelaces, they did. The old loafers re-emerged, transformed by the shoe repair shop, polished and with new heels. By the time the box came out again from under the bed, it was summer and the *zapatos* no longer fit my sister's feet.

It was not until years later that I figured out how my mother sometimes had her say, though when my father was in the room, I rarely heard her voice.

Much later, I watched my father prepare a care package for his family still in Cuba; they had requested toiletries, and the most sought-after item: *zapatos*. He had taken to wearing bulky sneakers, and he insisted on sending just that: "practical, sturdy shoes that kept feet firmly in place."

The heavy shoes he chose were a way of weighing himself down, secure to the ground. Like a paperweight on a string keeping a balloon from flying off, those *za-*

patos kept him tethered--tethered to his new land with all its strange ways, as if without them, he, too, would drift away.

I wonder if as a newcomer in the U.S., he imagined like Alice, a world of his own, where "nothing would be what it is because everything would be what it isn't."

About the Riversong Short Story Contest

The Riversong Short Story Contest aims to spotlight distinctive voices in the short story and poetry genres and provide a platform for emerging writers to showcase their talents in a published collection.

The contest operates annually, with the winners' collection published in October or November each year.

- Deadline: September 15th of each year
- Word limit: 10,000 words
- Genre and style: Any except erotica
- Entry fee: $29
- Winners announced: October 1st

You can submit your story anytime during the year, but submissions received after September 15th will be scheduled for the following year's contest.

Your manuscript will undergo a blind review by a panel of editors, bloggers, writers, and publishers. The focus is solely on the content and writing style of your story. The uniqueness of your story, voice, plot, and literary skill will help your story stand out.

All winners will be contacted privately, and their stories will be published in a volume of short stories in the fourth quarter of each year.

For more information and to enter the contest, visit https://sulisinternational.com/short-story-contest-landing/.

About the Publisher

Sulis International Press publishes select fiction and nonfiction in a variety of genres under four imprints: Riversong Books, Sulis Academic Press, Sulis Press, and Keledei Publications.

For more, visit the website at
https://sulisinternational.com

Subscribe to the newsletter at
https://sulisinternational.com/subscribe/

Follow on social media
https://www.facebook.com/SulisInternational
https://twitter.com/Sulis_Intl
https://www.pinterest.com/Sulis_Intl/
https://www.instagram.com/sulis_international/